A to Z Sign with Me
Sign Language for the Alphabet

by Dawn Babb Prochovnic
illustrated by Stephanie Bauer

Content Consultant:
Lora Heller, MS, MT-BC, LCAT
and Founding Director of Baby Fingers LLC

magic
Wagon

visit us at www.abdopublishing.com

For three AmaZing critique partners: Sara Behrman, Claire Horowitz and Becky Hawkins—DP
For the Bauer Girls, who are always up for a carnival....—SB

Published by Magic Wagon, a division of the ABDO Group, PO Box 398166, Minneapolis, Minnesota 55439.

Looking Glass Library™ is a trademark and logo of Magic Wagon.

Printed in the United States of America, North Mankato, Minnesota.
102011
012012
♻ This book contains at least 10% recycled materials.

Written by Dawn Babb Prochovnic
Illustrations by Stephanie Bauer
Edited by Stephanie Hedlund and Rochelle Baltzer
Cover and interior layout and design by Neil Klinepier

Story Time with Signs & Rhymes provides an introduction to ASL vocabulary through stories that are written and structured in English. ASL is a separate language with its own structure. Just as there are personal and regional variations in spoken and written languages, there are similar variations in sign language.

Library of Congress Cataloging-in-Publication Data

Prochovnic, Dawn Babb.
  A to Z sign with me : sign language for the alphabet / by Dawn Babb Prochovnic ; illustrated by Stephanie Bauer.
    p. cm. -- (Story time with signs & rhymes)
  Summary: Playful stories introduce the American Sign Language signs for animals, foods, and the different activities of a carnival.
  ISBN 978-1-61641-835-9
  1. Alphabet books. 2. American Sign Language--Juvenile fiction. 3. Stories in rhyme. 4. Animals--Juvenile fiction. 5. Carnivals--Juvenile fiction. [1. Sign language. 2. Alphabet. 3. Carnivals--Fiction. 4. Stories in rhyme.] I. Bauer, Stephanie, ill. II. Title. III. Series: Story time with signs & rhymes.
  PZ10.4.P76Aaj 2012
  [E]--dc23
                                                        2011027063

Alphabet Handshapes

American Sign Language (ASL) is a visual language that uses handshapes, movements, and facial expressions. Sometimes people spell English words by making the handshape for each letter in the word they want to sign. This is called fingerspelling. The pictures below show the handshapes for each letter in the manual alphabet.

Read along from **A** to **Z**.
Sign the handshapes that you see.

Aim for the **b**ull's-eye.
It's a **c**ircle and a **d**ot.

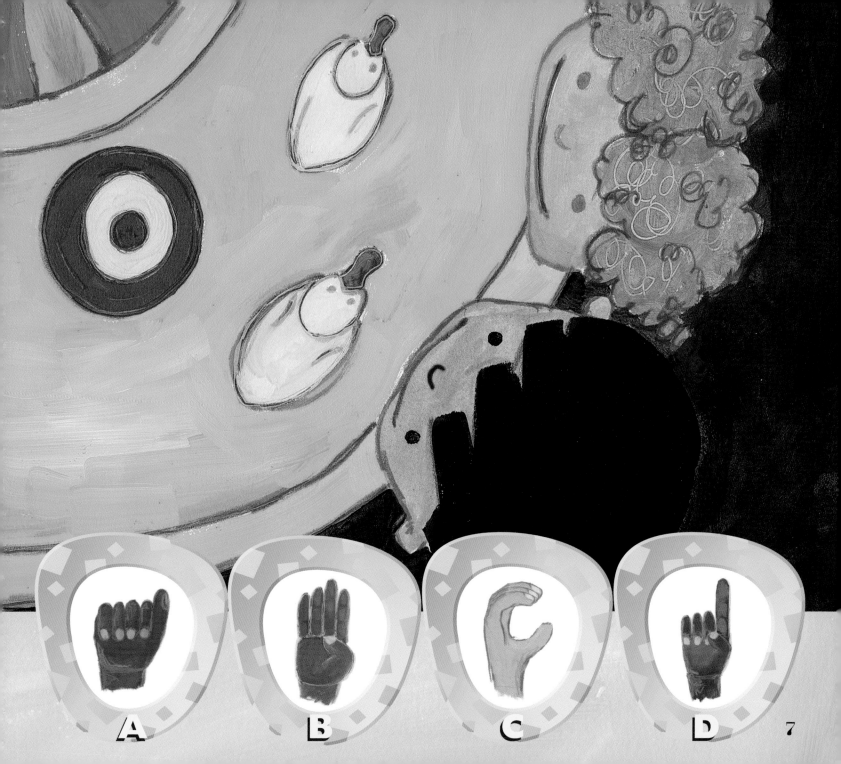

Eat frankfurters while they're good and hot.

E

F

G

H

9

Ice cream! Jelly beans! Kettle corn, please!

Lip grows a **m**ustache. **N**ose blows a sneeze.

ACHOO!!

L M N

13

Talk like the animals, "**O**ink! **P**eep! **Q**uack!"

15

Cheer when the **r**oller coaster **s**peeds down the **t**rack.

16

R   S   T

Look at the **u**nicycles rolling by.
See the **v**iew from the Ferris **w**heel in the sky.

18

U   V   W

Laugh as the clowns put on one last show.
Hunt for the exit. It's time to go.

X

Yay! That was fun. But, we're not done yet.

23

Zzz-Zzz. Now you've signed the alphabet!

American Sign Language Glossary

The alphabet handshapes can be signed with either the right or the left hand. Most people sign the alphabet with the hand they use to hold a pencil. This is called the dominant or active hand. The alphabet handshapes should be signed with the palm facing out, toward the person you are signing to.

Aa: Make a fist. The first knuckle on each finger should be flat. Your thumb should touch the side of your pointer finger and point up.

Bb: Point up with all four fingers, and bend your thumb at the large knuckle so it rests in your palm.

Cc: Curve your fingers and your thumb so it looks like the shape of the letter *C*.

Dd: Point up with your pointer finger. Curve your other three fingers down toward your thumb until the tip of your middle finger touches the tip of your thumb.

Ee: Bend your thumb at the large knuckle so it rests in your palm. Now bend all four fingers at the middle knuckle so your fingertips rest on the side of your thumb.

Ff: Curve your pointer finger down toward your thumb until your fingertip touches the tip of your thumb. Point up with your last three fingers.

Gg: Bend your last three fingers into the palm of your hand, and point to the side with your pointer finger and thumb.

Hh: Bend your last two fingers into the palm of your hand. Point to the side with your pointer finger and middle finger. Let your thumb rest on your bent fingers.

Ii: Use your thumb to bend your first three fingers into the palm of your hand. Point up with your pinkie finger.

Jj: Make the sign for the letter *I*, then use your pinkie finger to draw the hook shape of the letter *J* in the air.

Kk: Point up with your pointer finger, and point up and slightly forward with your middle finger. Rest your thumb between your pointer finger and middle finger, and bend your last two fingers into the palm of your hand.

Ll: Point up with your pointer finger and point to the side with your thumb. Bend your last three fingers into the palm of your hand. It should look like the shape of the letter *L*.

27

Mm: Use your thumb to bend your pinkie finger into the palm of your hand. Now bend your first three fingers over your thumb. The tip of your thumb should stick out between your third finger and your pinkie finger.

Nn: Use your thumb to bend your last two fingers into the palm of your hand. Now bend your first two fingers over your thumb. The tip of your thumb should stick out between your second and third fingers.

Oo: Curve all your fingers down until the tips of your fingers touch your thumb. It should look like the shape of the letter *O*.

Pp: Point out with your pointer finger, and point down and slightly toward your body with your middle finger. Rest your thumb between your pointer finger and middle finger, and bend your last two fingers into the palm of your hand. Hint: Make the sign for the letter *K*, but point your first two fingers out and down instead of pointing them up.

Qq: Bend your last three fingers into the palm of your hand, and point down with your pointer finger and thumb. Hint: Make the sign for the letter *G*, but point down with your pointer finger and thumb instead of to the side.

Rr: Use your thumb to bend your last two fingers into the palm of your hand. Cross your pointer and middle finger. Your pointer and middle finger should be pointing up.

Ss: Make a fist. Bend all your fingers into the palm of your hand, and bend your thumb at the large knuckle so that it rests across the front of your fingers.

Tt: Bend your last three fingers into the palm of your hand and rest your thumb on your middle finger. Now bend your pointer finger over your thumb. The tip of your thumb should point up from between your first two fingers.

 **Uu:** Use your thumb to bend your last two fingers into the palm of your hand. Hold your first two fingers together and point them up.

 **Vv:** Make the sign for the letter *U*, but spread your first two fingers apart. It should look like the shape of the letter *V*.

 Ww: Use your thumb to bend your pinkie finger into the palm of your hand. Spread your first three fingers apart and point them up. It should look like the shape of the letter *W*.

 Xx: Use your thumb to bend your last three fingers into the palm of your hand. Curve your pointer finger so your fingertip is pointing out.

 **Yy:** Bend your first three fingers down toward the palm of your hand while you stretch your thumb and pinkie finger out to each side. It should look like the shape of the letter *Y*.

 Zz: Use your thumb to bend your last three fingers into the palm of your hand. Use your pointer finger to make the shape of the letter *Z* in the air.

Fun Facts about ASL

Although there are ASL signs for many English words, some words do not have a sign. These words are fingerspelled. When you fingerspell, you make the handshape for each letter in the English word you want to sign. You can fingerspell any word you want to communicate, even if there is an ASL sign for that word. Fingerspelling can help you become a better speller, and it can be especially handy if you forget the sign for a word you are trying to communicate!

Proper names, such as Katie or Max, are often fingerspelled. A special tradition in the Deaf community is to give individuals a name sign. This is a unique sign that is created by someone in the Deaf community. It can be used in place of fingerspelling to identify an individual by name. It is generally considered disrespectful for people in the hearing community to create name signs for themselves or others.

When you know the handshape for each letter in the manual alphabet, it is easier to learn new signs in ASL. This is because some ASL signs incorporate the handshapes that are used to sign the manual alphabet. For example, the word *water* is signed by tapping the pointer finger of the "W Hand" on your chin.

Signing Activities

Alphabet Circle Game: Stand in a circle and choose someone to go first. The first player makes the sign for the letter *A*. The second player makes the sign for the letter *B*. Play continues with each player making the sign for the next letter in the alphabet until someone signs the letter that their name starts with. For example, if the letter *C* is signed by Cassi, play stops. This player must fingerspell their name and sit down. The player that goes next must start signing with the next letter in the alphabet. Play continues until everyone is sitting down. You will need to repeat the alphabet several times to finish the game.

Alphabet Song: Sing "The Alphabet Song" as you make the handshapes for the letters in the manual alphabet. Try this again, but this time, sing faster. Now try it again, but this time, make the alphabet handshapes with both your right and your left hand. Now that's tricky!

Alphabet Guessing Game: This is a fun game for partners. Take turns being the signer. The first signer makes the handshape for one of the letters in the manual alphabet. The partner makes the sound that is made by that letter of the alphabet. When the partner makes the correct sound, switch roles. Continue taking turns until you and your partner have correctly made the handshapes and sounds for each letter of the alphabet.

Additional Resources

Further Reading

Coleman, Rachel. *Once Upon a Time* (Signing Time DVD, Series 2, Volume 11). Two Little Hands Productions, 2008.

Edge, Nellie. *ABC Phonics: Sing, Sign, and Read!* Northlight Communications, 2010.

Heller, Lora. *Sign Language for Kids.* Sterling, 2004.

Valli, Clayton. *The Gallaudet Dictionary of American Sign Language.* Gallaudet University Press, 2005.

Web Sites

To learn more about ASL, visit ABDO Group online at **www.abdopublishing.com**. Web sites about ASL are featured on our Book Links page. These links are routinely monitored and updated to provide the most current information available.